Wise Owl's
BOOK OF SOUNDS

by Jane Belk Moncure
illustrated by Helen Endres
created by Child's World

 CHILDRENS PRESS, CHICAGO

Library of Congress Cataloging in Publication Data

Moncure, Jane Belk.
    Wise Owl's book of sounds.

    (Wise Owl plus)
    Summary: Wise Owl helps Little Owl identify
the sounds of the night.
    [1. Sound — Fiction.   2. Owls — Fiction.
3. Night — Fiction]   I. Endres, Helen, ill.
II. Title.
PZ7.M739Wht   [E]   81-18094
ISBN 0-516-06564-5   AACR2

Wise Owl had a problem.

"There is too much noise in this house," he said. "I need some QUIET."

"If the little ones had a special place to play, it would be more quiet," said Mrs. Owl.

Little Owl beat his drum.

"TUM-TUM-TUM!"

Baby Owl marched to the drumbeat. She tooted her horn.

"TOOT-TOOT-TOOT!"

But she did not see the table.

"BOOM! CRASH!"

All the dishes crashed to the floor.

Wise Owl jumped up. "That does it!" he shouted. "I must do something about this!"

Wise Owl sat back down. He thought and thought.

"I know!" he said at last. "I'll build a tree house. Then the kids will play outside more. And I will have QUIET."

Wise Owl went right to work. He used a
hammer and nails, a saw and some wood. He
worked until dark.

He built a fine tree house.

"Tomorrow you can play in your own special place," said Wise Owl to Little Owl.

"How about tonight?" asked Little Owl. "May I camp out tonight?"

"The other boys are not here," said Mrs. Owl. "I do not want you out alone."

"Nights are so quiet around here," said Wise Owl. "I'll camp out with Little Owl tonight."

"Wow," said Little Owl. He ran and got his sleeping bag.

Soon Wise Owl and Little Owl were snuggled inside their sleeping bags. They could see the stars.

"The night seems quiet," whispered Wise Owl. "But still there are sounds all around us. Let's see who can guess the sounds of the night."

Little Owl listened.

"OOO-OOO-H! OOO-OOO-H!"

"What was that?" Wise Owl asked.

"I don't see anything," said Little Owl.

"Some things you can hear but not see," said Wise Owl.

"OOO-OOO-H! OOO-OOO-H!" came the sound again. The tree house swayed just a little.

"Oh, now I know," said Little Owl. "It is the wind."

"Right," said Wise Owl. "Listen again."

"CRACK! BA-BOOM!"

Little Owl heard a sharp cracking sound. Then he heard a rumbling. "That is thunder! There must be a storm coming," he said.

"Must be," said Wise Owl.

"Let's listen some more," said Little Owl.

Everything was still. Then,
"RIB-IT! RIB-IT!"

"What was that? Is it Grandfather Owl practicing his banjo?" asked Little Owl.

"No, it is Frog singing a song," laughed Wise Owl.

It was very quiet. Then,
"SPLISH-SPLASH!"

"What was that? Is Baby Owl taking a bath?"
asked Little Owl.

"No. Beaver is taking a swim in the pond,"
laughed Wise Owl.

"ZOOM, ZOOM!"

"I know what that is," said Little Owl. "That's a jet."

"Right," said Wise Owl. "Now, let's get some sleep."

Little Owl turned over. Soon he heard,
"DRIP! DROP! DRIP!"

"I hear rain!" he said.

"Get inside your sleeping bag," said Wise Owl.

It was dark inside the sleeping bag. Little Owl
could not see, but he could hear.

"CRICK–ET! CRICK–ET! CRICK–ET!"

Little Owl knew that sound.

"BONG! BONG! BONG! . . ."

The grandfather clock in the hall chimed twelve o'clock. Little Owl heard it through the open window.

Then from far away came a howling noise.

"AHOOOOOO! AHOOOOOO!"

"That's a wolf," Little Owl said.

"Go to sleep," said Wise Owl.

Little Owl did. Then there were no sounds at all
until . . . "COCK-A-DOODLE-DOO!"

The rooster down the road was awake.

Little Owl heard the rooster. "It's morning," he said.

"SIZZLE-POP!"

"Do I hear bacon frying?" asked Wise Owl. He was not quite awake.

"It's breakfast!" shouted Little Owl.

Mrs. Owl brought breakfast outside.

"The night was full of sounds," said Little Owl. He took his fifth pancake.

"But I still slept," said Wise Owl. He took his tenth pancake.

"SHU-BANG! VAROOM!"

Big Brother Owl and Middle Brother Owl drove up on their trail bikes.

Then they saw the tree house!

"Just the place to practice my tuba," said Big Brother.

"Just the place to play my guitar," said Middle Brother.

"Just the place to play my drums," said Little Owl.

". . . and my horn!" said Baby Owl.

Suddenly they heard a siren.

"ErrrrRRRRRrrrrr!"

A fire truck raced down the road.

Wise Owl hurried inside the house. He closed all the windows. He locked all the doors.

Then he sat in his chair and put a pillow on his head.

In a little while, Wise Owl did not hear a sound!

A Wise Owl Plus

Wise Owl did not like loud sounds. But he did like quiet sounds.

Here are some sounds you might hear. Are they loud sounds or quiet sounds?

horn tooting

dishes crashing

fan blowing

cat lapping

balloon popping

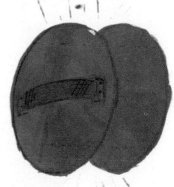

cymbals crashing

loudspeaker blaring

water running